MW01041143

This book is presented to:

....

Luke 1:26-38, Matthew 1:18-24
Luke 2:1-20, Matthew 2:1-11

Introduce your little ones to the true meaning of Christmas with our Nativity Story Advent Calendar. This calendar is designed to bring your family together for an experiential journey through the Advent season.

Within the calendar, you'll discover 25 days of family activities to help you countdown to Christmas Day. Each page offers:

- 25 Days of Family Reading of THE NATIVITY STORY
- 25 Days of CHRISTMAS ACTS OF KINDNESS
- 25 Days of Preparation for the FAMILY NATIVITY PLAY

Simply read each day's Nativity story and engage in these family Advent activities together.

The Nativity Story and the Nativity Play Script are adapted and quoted from the Holy Bible, the International Children's Bible (ICB), the Easy-to-Read Version (ERV), and the New American Bible Revised Edition (NABRE).

MamTalk
BOOKS FOR KIDS

Day 1

25 Days of Family Reading
OF THE NATIVITY STORY

This story begins about 2000 years ago in Nazareth, a little town filled with shepherds and farmers. In this town lived a kind young woman named Mary.

25 Days of Christmas
ACTS OF KINDNESS

Spread kindness and cheer to people every day, especially in anticipation of Christmas!

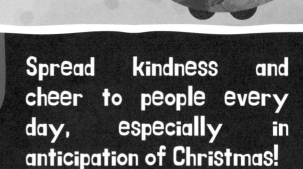

Day 1:
Introduction and Casting

25 Days of Preparation for the
FAMILY NATIVITY PLAY

Please find the Family Nativity Play Script at the end of the book. Gather the family and introduce the Nativity play project. Read the Nativity play script together.

Day 2

Mary was going to marry a kind and honest man named Joseph. A few days before the engagement, Mary had a very special visitor.

Make Christmas cards and distribute them to the elderly at a retirement home.

25 Days of Christmas
ACTS OF KINDNESS

25 Days of Preparation for the
FAMILY NATIVITY PLAY

Day 2:
Introduction and Casting

Discuss which family members will play which roles. Roles for 1st and 2nd Narrators are recommended for adults.

FAMILY Activities to Countdown to Christmas DAY

This very special visitor was the angel Gabriel sent by God from heaven. He wore a bright white robe and had big silver wings.

25 Days of Christmas
ACTS OF KINDNESS

Spend time with your grandparents. Make gingerbread house together.

FAMILY Activities to Countdown to Christmas DAY

Day 3:
Introduction and Casting

Assign roles to participants for Mary, Joseph, Angels, Shepherds, Wise Men, Narrators, Donkey, and Sheep.

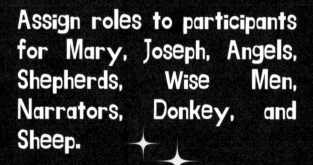

25 Days of Preparation for the
FAMILY NATIVITY PLAY

Day 4

The angel Gabriel told Mary she would have a baby boy and would name him Jesus. He will be called the Son of God.

25 Days of Christmas
ACTS OF KINDNESS

Make a family member breakfast in bed.

25 Days of Preparation for the
FAMILY NATIVITY PLAY

Day 4:
Costume Planning

Begin planning and organizing costumes for each character. List what items are needed for each costume. Check for items you already have at home.

FAMILY Activities to Countdown to Christmas DAY

Day 5

25 Days of Family Reading
OF THE NATIVITY STORY

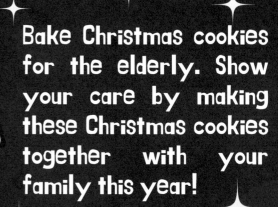

The angel appeared to Joseph in a dream. He said that Mary's baby is from God and that Joseph should take care of both Mary and the baby.

25 Days of Christmas
ACTS OF KINDNESS

Bake Christmas cookies for the elderly. Show your care by making these Christmas cookies together with your family this year!

Day 5:
Costume Creation

25 Days of Preparation for the
FAMILY NATIVITY PLAY

Create a costume for angels—the tunics in white with wings made of cardboard and nimbuses made of wire and tinsel.

FAMILY Activities to Countdown to Christmas DAY

25 Days of Family Reading
OF THE NATIVITY STORY

Day 6

In those days, the king of the country wanted to count how many people lived there, so Mary and Joseph had to travel to Bethlehem.

25 Days of Christmas
ACTS OF KINDNESS

Read or tell the Nativity story to your younger siblings at bedtime.

25 Days of Preparation for the
FAMILY NATIVITY PLAY

Day 6:
Costume Creation

Make a costume for Mary and Joseph using the costume suggestions in the Nativity Play Script.

FAMILY Activities to Countdown to Christmas DAY

Day 7

When they arrived in Bethlehem, all the hotels were full. The only place they could find to stay was a barn where the animals lived.

25 Days of Christmas
ACTS OF KINDNESS

Compliment your neighbor's holiday decorations and brights.

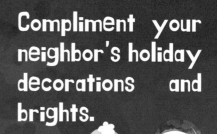

Day 7:
Costume Creation

25 Days of Preparation for the
FAMILY NATIVITY PLAY

Make costumes for two Shepherds and three Wise Men using the costume suggestions in the Nativity Play Script.

FAMILY Activities to Countdown to Christmas DAY

25 Days of Family Reading
OF THE NATIVITY STORY

In the night, something magical happened. Mary gave birth to Jesus, a beautiful baby boy. Mary and Joseph laid him to sleep in a manger.

Clean up your toys and books without being asked to.

25 Days of Christmas
ACTS OF KINDNESS

25 Days of Preparation for the
FAMILY NATIVITY PLAY

Day 8:
Costume Creation

Make costumes for Donkey and Sheep using the costume suggestions. Cut the paper masks for them out of the page at the end of the book.

FAMILY Activities to Countdown to Christmas DAY

Day 9

Jesus was born among the animals. Mary was happy that the Angels' predictions had come true. Jesus Christ, the Savior of this world, was born in a humble manger.

25 Days of Christmas
ACTS OF KINDNESS

Offer compliments to friends, family, and strangers.

You are kind!

You are smart!

You are beautiful!

You are tallented!

Day 9:
Costume Finalization

Finish creating or altering costumes. Ensure that all costumes are ready.

25 Days of Preparation for the
FAMILY NATIVITY PLAY

Day 10

Not very far from Bethlehem, some shepherds were looking after their sheep on a hill when, suddenly, an angel appeared.

Spend time with your family and decorate the outside of your house together.

25 Days of Christmas
ACTS OF KINDNESS

25 Days of Preparation for the
FAMILY NATIVITY PLAY

Day 10:
Set Design

Discuss and plan the set for your Nativity play. Determine what materials are needed. Use suggestions for sets in the Nativity Play Script.

FAMILY Activities to Countdown to Christmas DAY

Day 11

The angel said, "Don't be afraid! I bring good news about Jesus' birth! You will find him lying in a manger!"

FAMILY Activities to Countdown to Christmas DAY

25 Days of Christmas
ACTS OF KINDNESS

Draw a card for your teacher, friend, neighbor, firefighter, policeman, or mail carrier.

Day 11:
Set Construction

Start building the play's set and assign tasks to family members. Create a stable roof and a large Christmas star using cardboard.

25 Days of Preparation for the
FAMILY NATIVITY PLAY

25 Days of Family Reading
OF THE NATIVITY STORY

Day 12

Suddenly there was a multitude of the heavenly host with the angel, praising God.

25 Days of Christmas
ACTS OF KINDNESS

Peace, joy, and blessing!

Collect warm clothes that no longer fit and donate them.

25 Days of Preparation for the
FAMILY NATIVITY PLAY

Day 12:
Set Finalization

Complete the construction and decoration of the set, including crafting a manger from a cardboard box.

FAMILY Activities to Countdown to Christmas DAY

Day 13

25 Days of Family Reading
OF THE NATIVITY STORY

The shepherds hurried to Bethlehem and found Mary, Joseph, and baby Jesus. They shared what the angels had said about this child, and everyone was surprised.

25 Days of Christmas
ACTS OF KINDNESS

Call family members to say "hi" and tell them about your day.

Day 13:
Rehearsal – Scene 1

25 Days of Preparation for the
FAMILY NATIVITY PLAY

Start rehearsing Scene 1 with the cast. Focus on lines, movements, and timing.

FAMILY Activities to Countdown to Christmas DAY

The shepherds returned to their sheep, praising and thanking God. It was just as the angel had told them.

25 Days of Christmas
ACTS OF KINDNESS

Purchase or make small, thoughtful Christmas gifts for your siblings.

25 Days of Preparation for the
FAMILY NATIVITY PLAY

Day 14:
Rehearsal - Scene 2

Start rehearsing Scene 2 with the cast. Continue to refine lines and actions.

Day 15

In a land far away, three wise men saw a bright star in the sky. They knew it meant a special king was born.

FAMILY Activities to Countdown to Christmas DAY

25 Days of Christmas
ACTS OF KINDNESS

Donate your toys to kids in need. Find at least five things that are in good condition for a child who doesn't have as many toys.

Day 15:
Rehearsal - Scene 3

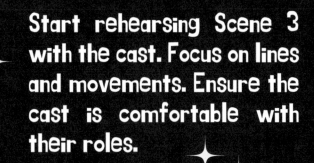

Start rehearsing Scene 3 with the cast. Focus on lines and movements. Ensure the cast is comfortable with their roles.

25 Days of Preparation for the
FAMILY NATIVITY PLAY

25 Days of Family Reading
OF THE NATIVITY STORY

Day 16

The wise men followed the star for several days until it stopped right over the manger.

Make a Bird feeder together with your parents, grandparents, or Godparents.

25 Days of Christmas
ACTS OF KINDNESS

25 Days of Preparation for the
FAMILY NATIVITY PLAY

Day 16:
Rehearsal – Scene 4

Start rehearsing Scene 4 with the cast. Continue to refine lines and actions. Work on transitions between scenes.

FAMILY Activities to Countdown to Christmas DAY

25 Days of Family Reading
OF THE NATIVITY STORY

The wise men bowed down to Jesus and gave him special gifts of gold, frankincense, and myrrh.

25 Days of Christmas
ACTS OF KINDNESS

Make hot chocolate for your family on a cold day.

Day 17:
Rehearsal - Scene 5

25 Days of Preparation for the
FAMILY NATIVITY PLAY

Start rehearsing Scene 5 with the cast. Focus on lines, movements, and interactions between characters.

Day 18

These were gifts given only to kings. The wise men knew that Jesus was a very special king, the Son of God, and the Savior of the world.

25 Days of Christmas
ACTS OF KINDNESS

Donate food to a food bank. Help your parents clear out the pantry and donate some of your canned goods to a food bank.

25 Days of Preparation for the
FAMILY NATIVITY PLAY

Day 18:
Rehearsal - Scene 6

Start rehearsing Scene 6 with the cast. Continue to refine lines and actions. Make sure everyone knows their cues.

Mary and Joseph were thankful to God for all their visitors — the shepherds and the wise men.

25 Days of Christmas
ACTS OF KINDNESS

Perform a concert for the elderly at a retirement home.

Day 19:
Rehearsal - Scene 7

25 Days of Preparation for the
FAMILY NATIVITY PLAY

Start rehearsing Scene 7 with the cast. And also run through the entire play. Focus on lines and movements.

25 Days of Family Reading
OF THE NATIVITY STORY

Day 20

FAMILY Activities to Countdown to Christmas DAY

Mary was filled with joy because the predictions of the angel Gabriel had come true.

Thank a teacher with a gift made with your own hands.

25 Days of Christmas
ACTS OF KINDNESS

25 Days of Preparation for the
FAMILY NATIVITY PLAY

Day 20:
Costume Rehearsal

Have a costume rehearsal to ensure everyone is comfortable in their outfits.

Day 21

The town of Bethlehem was filled with love and hope because of baby Jesus, the Son of God and the Savior of the world, who began His journey on Earth. He came to bring people love, joy, faith, and hope!

FAMILY Activities to Countdown to Christmas DAY

25 Days of Christmas
ACTS OF KINDNESS

Write letters or draw pictures for soldiers and wish them a Merry Christmas.

Day 21:
Set Dress Rehearsal

25 Days of Preparation for the
FAMILY NATIVITY PLAY

Perform a rehearsal with the full set to work out any issues.

25 Days of Family Reading
OF THE NATIVITY STORY

Day 22

As Jesus grew, He performed many miracles, including healing the sick, feeding with five loaves, restoring sight to the blind, walking on water, and even raising people from the dead.

Make Christmas decorations and take them to a children's hospital to please sick kids.

25 Days of Christmas
ACTS OF KINDNESS

25 Days of Preparation for the
FAMILY NATIVITY PLAY

Day 22:
Technical Rehearsal

Run through the play with lighting, sound, and props.

FAMILY Activities to Countdown to Christmas DAY

FAMILY Activities to Countdown to Christmas DAY

EVERY DAY
GOD THINKS OF YOU!
Jeremiah 29:11
EVERY MINUTE
GOD CARES FOR YOU!
1 Peter 5:7
BECAUSE EVERY SECOND
HE LOVES YOU!
1 John 4:16

His love is still with us today, bringing joy to our hearts!

25 Days of Christmas
ACTS OF KINDNESS

Feliz Navidad

Learn to say "Merry Christmas!" in different languages to different people.

Day 23:
Invitations to the Nativity Play

Prepare and distribute invitations to the Nativity Play.

25 Days of Preparation for the
FAMILY NATIVITY PLAY

25 Days of Family Reading
OF THE NATIVITY STORY

On Christmas Eve, we celebrate the birth of Jesus, the greatest gift of all!

Take cookies to a fire station to thank the firefighters for their work tonight, and then attend midnight mass at church with your family.

25 Days of Christmas
ACTS OF KINDNESS

25 Days of Preparation for the
FAMILY NATIVITY PLAY

Day 24:
Installation of Stage Sets and Final Rehearsal

Perform a dress rehearsal with costumes, set, and props. Make any last-minute adjustments.

FAMILY Activities to Countdown to Christmas DAY

Now you know the Bible story of Jesus' birth! The birth of Jesus is the true reason why we celebrate Christmas!

MERRY CHRISTMAS

25 Days of Christmas
ACTS OF KINDNESS

Donate some of your Christmas gifts to an orphanage.

Day 25: Play Day

The big day has arrived! Perform your Family Nativity Play. Enjoy your Nativity Play, and have a fantastic holiday season!

25 Days of Preparation for the
FAMILY NATIVITY PLAY

The Nativity Play Script

Cast of characters

Narrator 1
Narrator 2
Angel
Joseph
Mary
Donkey

Other Angels (2 or more)
Choir (all actors and audiences)

Shepherd 1
Shepherd 2
Wise man 1
Wise man 2
Wise man 3
Sheep

Suggestions for costumes

For creating costumes, you can use dad's t-shirts or shirts, mom's blouses or tunics, and scarves. Another option is to craft costumes for all participants from plain pillowcases. Simply cut the pillowcase along two of the longer sides and make a hole for the head on the shorter side. Participants can then put on these improvised tunics and tie them with a rope at the waist. For the headpiece, use a scarf tied with a rope.

Specific costume instructions for each character:

Mary: A tunic and headpiece in white or blue. Mary has a baby doll and a blanket hidden in the manger.

Joseph: A tunic and headpiece in brown, navy, or gray. Joseph can hold a long stick.

Two Shepherds: A tunic and headpiece in beige or gray. Shepherds can hold long sticks.

Angels: A tunic in white with wings made of cardboard. For the headpiece, use a nimbus made of wire and tinsel.

Three Wise Men: A robe or tunic in bright colors such as crimson, purple, or gold. For the headpiece, use a turban or crown. Wise Men have three gifts.

Donkey: Gray clothing and paper mask.

Sheep: White clothing and paper mask. (Cut it out of the pages at the end of the book.)

Suggestions for sets

To create the stable, you just need a roof. It can be made from two large pieces of cardboard, forming a triangular space. Place a large paper Christmas Star above the roof. Decorate the stable area with stuffed animals, and position a cardboard box to serve as the manger.

Scene 1: The Angel and Mary (Luke 1:26-38)

The stage is dark. Narrator 1 begins speaking.
During the performance, two Narrators stand STAGE LEFT.
Illuminate the Narrators whenever they speak, and lower
the light when they stop talking.

Narrator 1: Christmas is celebrated all over the world. It marks the birth of Jesus Christ, the Messiah and the Son of God. This is the greatest story ever told—the story of the first Christmas. It is the story of God's own Son coming into the world to save us.

Narrator 2: This story begins about 2000 years ago in Nazareth, a little town filled with shepherds and farmers. In this town lived a young woman named Mary. Mary was going to marry a kind and honest man named Joseph. Mary was special, very kind, and loved God very much; that is why God had chosen her to be the Mother of His Only Son. God sent an angel named Gabriel to Mary.

Lights come up on Mary and Angel, who are standing STAGE RIGHT.

Angel: Greetings Mary! God is with you! Soon you will have a son, and you will name him Jesus. He will be called the Son of God and the Savior of the world!

Mary: I trust God, so let it happen as God wants!

The lights dim on Mary and Angel, and they exit STAGE RIGHT.

Scene 2: The Angel and Joseph (Matthew 1:18-24)

Lights come up on Joseph and Angel, who are standing STAGE RIGHT.
Joseph is "sleeping" (he stands with his eyes closed and snores, with
two palms together under his ear to show he's sleeping).

Joseph: Z-z-z-z-z-z-z

Narrator 1: One night, the angel of God appeared to Joseph in a dream.

Angel: Joseph, Mary is going to have a child. Her child is holy and will be the Son of God! You will name him Jesus. Take Mary, your wife, into your home.

Narrator 2: Joseph accepted everything required by the angel of God.

Angel exits STAGE RIGHT, and Joseph "wakes up."

Joseph: I will take Mary as my wife and raise this child as my own son.

Joseph exits STAGE RIGHT. Lights dim.

Scene 3: Travel to Bethlehem (Luke 2:1-5)

Narrator 1: In those days, the king of the country wanted to count how many people lived there. Everyone was required to go to their hometown to register.

Narrator 2: So, Joseph and Mary, who was pregnant, had to travel from Nazareth to Bethlehem.

*Lights come up on Mary, Joseph, and Donkey,
who are standing STAGE LEFT.*

Joseph: Mary, we must travel to Bethlehem on a donkey.

Donkey: Bray, Bray to the little town of Bethlehem!

*Choir sings 'O Little Town of Bethlehem' as Mary, Joseph, and Donkey
walk slowly from STAGE LEFT to STAGE RIGHT. The lights dim on
Mary, Joseph, and Donkey.*

Choir (all actors and audiences):
O little town of Bethlehem,
how still we see thee lie!
Above thy deep and dreamless sleep,
the silent stars go by.

Scene 4: The Birth of Jesus (Luke 2:6-7)

*Lights come up on Mary, Joseph, and Donkey,
who are standing STAGE RIGHT.*

Narrator 1: When Joseph and Mary came to Bethlehem, all the hotels were full.

Mary: Joseph, there is no room at the hotels.

Joseph: We will have to stay in a stable with the animals.

*Mary and Joseph walk from STAGE RIGHT
to the stable area STAGE CENTER.*

Narrator 2: That night, Mary gave birth to a son. She wrapped him in swaddling clothes and laid him in a manger.

*While the narrator speaks, Mary swaddles the baby
doll in a blanket and gently lays it in the manger.
Mary and Joseph kneel beside the manger.*

Mary: I will call him Jesus, as the angel told me!

Joseph: He is the promised Messiah, the Son of God!

Choir (all actors and audiences):
Away in a manger, no crib for a bed,
the little Lord Jesus laid down His sweet head;
the stars in the bright sky looked down where He lay,
the little Lord Jesus asleep on the hay.

*Choir sings, and lights are dimmed
on the stable scene.*

Scene 5: The Angel and Shepherds (Luke 2:8-14)

Lights come up on Angel, two Shepherds, and Sheep, who are standing STAGE RIGHT.

Narrator 1: Not very far from Bethlehem, some shepherds were looking over their flock. The angel of God appeared to them. The shepherds were terrified.

Shepherd 1: Are you the Messenger of God?

Shepherd 2: Why did you come?

Angel: Do not be afraid; I bring good news about the birth of the Son of God! You will find him wrapped in swaddling clothes and lying in a manger.

Narrator 2: Suddenly, a very large group of angels from heaven joined the first angel, praising God.

Angel 2, Angel 3, ... come on stage. Lights come up on all Angels.

All Angels: Glory to God in the highest, and on earth peace among men!

Angels, Shepherds, and Sheep: Hark! the herald angels sing…

Choir (all actors and audiences):
Hark! the herald angels sing,
"Glory to the newborn King:
peace on earth, and mercy mild,
God and sinners reconciled!"
Joyful, all ye nations, rise,
join the triumph of the skies;
with th'angelic hosts proclaim,
"Christ is born in Bethlehem!"
Hark! the herald angels sing,
"Glory to the newborn King!"

All Angels and Sheep exit STAGE RIGHT. Lights dim.

Scene 6: The Visit of the Shepherds (Luke 2:15-20)

Lights come up on two Shepherds, who are standing STAGE RIGHT.

Narrator 1: When the angels left the shepherds and went back to heaven, the shepherds said to each other:

Shepherd 1: Let us go to Bethlehem to see this baby!

Shepherds walk from STAGE RIGHT to the stable area STAGE CENTER. Lights come up on the stable.

Shepherd 2: We have come to worship the King and Savior of the world.

The Shepherds bow to Jesus and exit STAGE LEFT.

Scene 7: The Visit of the Wise Men (Matthew 2:1-11)

*Lights come up on all three Wise Men, who are standing STAGE RIGHT.
As the Narrators speak, the three Wise Men walk slowly from
STAGE RIGHT to the stable area at CENTER STAGE.
They raise their hands and point to a large star on the stable.*

Narrator 1: Far away, wise men saw the new star. They knew it was a sign that the Savior had been born. They followed the star for several days until it stopped right over the manger. They saw the child with his mother, Mary, and they bowed down and worshipped him.

Narrator 2: Then they opened their treasures and offered Him gifts of gold, frankincense, and myrrh to show that baby Jesus is a special King, the Son of God, and the Savior of the world. These were gifts given only to kings.

Wise Man 1: We are Wise Men from the East. We have traveled a long way, guided by a bright star, to find your child and bring him gifts. I brought the gift of gold.

Wise Man 2: I have brought the child the gift of frankincense.

Wise Man 3: I have brought the child the gift of myrrh.

Mary: Thank you for these gifts. May God bless you and keep you safe on your journey!

Choir (all actors and audiences):

We three kings of Orient are;
bearing gifts we traverse afar,
field and fountain, moor and mountain,
following yonder star.

Narrator 1: This was the first Christmas. Now you know the story of Jesus' birth and how the Savior of the world began His journey on Earth.

Narrator 2: Jesus came to our world to bring love, hope, and salvation to all, to teach us to be kind, and to share His message of peace and joy.

All actors and audiences sing the final song, 'Joy to the World'.

During the final song 'Joy to the World', all participants make their way up to the front of the room and take their bows.

Choir (all actors and audiences):

Joy to the world, the Lord is come!
Let earth receive her King!
Let every heart prepare Him room,
and heaven and nature sing,
and heaven and nature sing,
and heaven, and heaven and nature sing.

THE END!

Merry Christmas!
Thank you for reading!

If you enjoyed our Nativity Story Advent Calendar, please check out our other popular books.

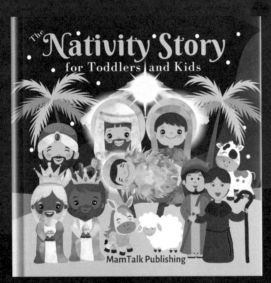

ASIN: B09LWH2B79

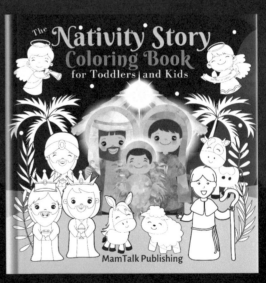

ASIN: B09MBZM8NR

If you can spare a few minutes to leave us a review, we'd be super grateful!

BOOKS FOR KIDS

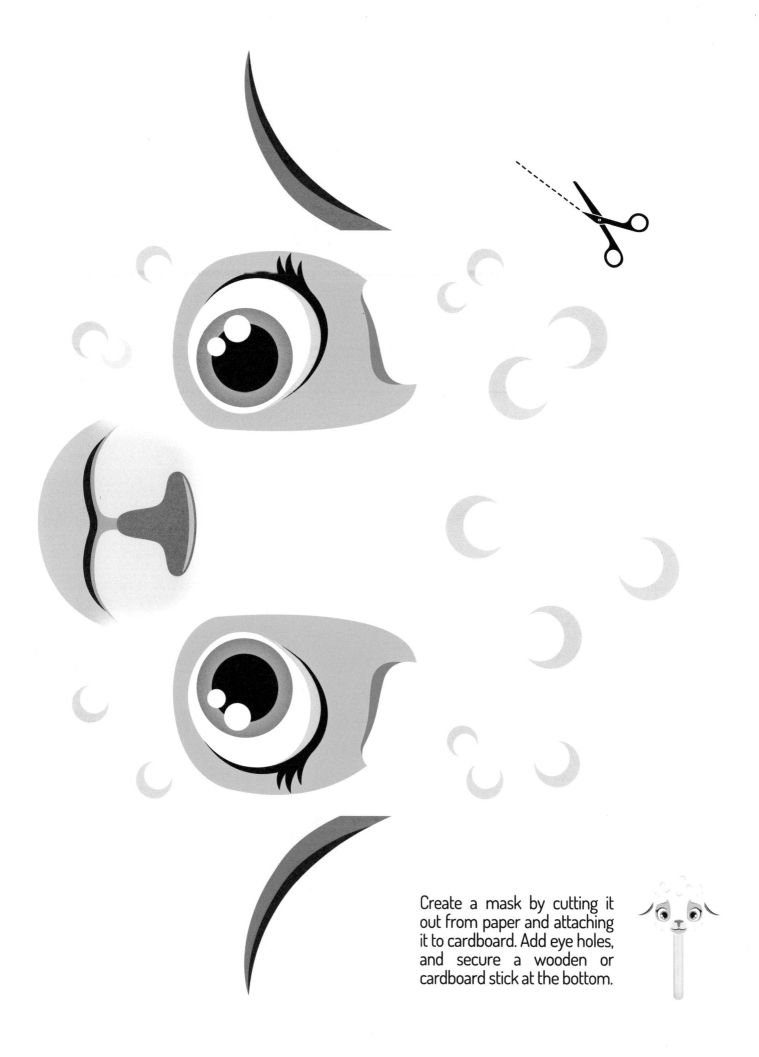

Create a mask by cutting it out from paper and attaching it to cardboard. Add eye holes, and secure a wooden or cardboard stick at the bottom.

Create a mask by cutting it out from paper and attaching it to cardboard. Add eye holes, and secure a wooden or cardboard stick at the bottom.

Made in United States
Troutdale, OR
11/25/2023

14946363R00024